Raggedy Ann's Magical Wishes

Raggedy Ann's Magical Wishes

By JOHNNY GRUELLE

Illustrated by the author

COLLINS · LONDON AND GLASGOW

ISBN 0-00-120444-0

PRINTED IN GREAT BRITAIN BY WILLIAM COLLINS SONS & CO LTD,
Glasgow

TO TWO LITTLE PLAYMATES
TEDDY G— and DICKIE G—

CHAPTER ONE

Little Neepy

ONE day, when the real-for-sure folks had gone away from home and Raggedy Ann and Raggedy Andy had been left out in the little play-house in the orchard, Raggedy Ann said to Raggedy Andy, "Raggedy Andy, do you know what?"

"No, what?" Raggedy Andy asked in reply.

"Well sir!" Raggedy Ann smiled, "My magical Wishing Pebble which I have safe and sound, sewed up inside my cotton-stuffed body, is jiggling around!"

Raggedy Andy got to his wabbly cloth feet and stumped over to Raggedy Ann. "Let me see, Raggedy Ann!" he said, as he felt Raggedy Ann's cotton-stuffed body with his rag hands. "Yes sir!" he laughed, "I can feel it jiggling around, Raggedy Ann. What do you s'pose can be the trouble with it?"

"Maybe it wants me to make a wish!" Raggedy Ann said; "I haven't made a wish for the longest, longest time, you know."

"I know it, Raggedy Ann!" Raggedy Andy said. "It seems ages and ages since we have had a lovely adventure! Do you s'pect we could have one today?"

"I s'pect we could, Raggedy Andy!" Raggedy Ann replied. "Marcella has forgotten she put us out here in the play-house and I am sure all the folks, even Dinah, the cook, have gone away!"

"Why not make a wish to know when they will return?" Raggedy Andy asked. "Then," he continued, "we would know just how long we could have to hunt for an adventure!"

"That is a good idea, Raggedy Andy!" Raggedy Ann laughed. "Now remain real quiet and we shall soon see if the Wishing Pebble is as good as it used to be, or whether it has lost its magical power!"

Raggedy Andy remained real quiet, though he was very anxious.

He sat down beside Raggedy Ann.

Raggedy Ann smoothed out the wrinkles in her pretty white apron and covered both shoe-button eyes with her rag hands. Not that she had to do this when she made a wish with the magical Wishing Pebble. Oh, no! But Raggedy Ann covered her shoe-button eyes with her hands so that if there was any magic to be seen, she would see it in this manner.

"Aha! Raggedy Andy!" Raggedy Ann finally said, as she took her hands from her shoe-button eyes, "when I wished to know how long the folks would be away from home, I saw, just as if it were written in golden letters on a piece of paper, the words, 'Long enough.' So I s'pect we can start right out and hunt an adventure!"

Raggedy Andy hopped to his feet and ran to the little window in the play-house. He looked across the orchard towards the deep, deep woods. Then he ran to the door and looked out in that direction.

There was no one in sight. Old Bossy, the cow, was standing, sleepy-eyed, over in one corner of the field, but cows did not count.

Since it was broad daylight, with the sun shining brightly, the Raggedys wanted to be certain that no real-for-sure person was about to watch them leave. "I cannot see any-one, either coming down the road, or crossing the fields— or anywhere!" Raggedy Andy said, as he helped Raggedy Ann to her feet. Raggedy Andy always believed in being polite, and, as you very well know, it is always polite for a boy to help a girl in every possible way.

The Raggedys, holding hands, raced across the orchard towards the fence. Old Bossy opened her eyes in amazement to see the Raggedy dolls running as they did, but Bossy did not say anything.

When they reached the fence, Raggedy Andy helped Raggedy Ann through, for it was an old-fashioned wooden fence; then he climbed through himself.

They scampered through some ferns and in a short time came to a lovely smooth path.

"I wish we had roller skates or something, so that we could just go scooting along the smooth path!" Raggedy Andy said.

"Wait a moment!" Raggedy Ann cried as she came to a stop. "Let's wish for something, Raggedy Andy! What do you say if I make a wish for two magical bicycles? The kind that will run by themselves without working our feet!"

"Ooh! That would be lovely, Raggedy Ann!" Raggedy Andy clapped his hands together and danced up and down at the thought.

"And all we shall have to do will be to jump on the bicycles and wish them to go and they will run by themselves! Oh! I think I shall wish for them right away, Raggedy Andy!"

"Please do, Raggedy Ann!" Raggedy Andy cried.

So Raggedy Ann made the wish, and before you could say Higgledy Piggledy backwards, there stood two beautiful, shiny red bicycles with chromium-plated handle-bars, pedals and rubber tyres and shiny bells and everything.

"How lovely!" Raggedy Andy cried, his little shoe-button eyes dancing with excitement.

"And thanks so much for making my wish come true, nice magical Wishing Pebble!" Raggedy Ann said as she patted the spot in her rag body where the Pebble was sewn!

Raggedy Andy helped Raggedy Ann upon her bicycle,

then he climbed upon his own and as soon as the Raggedys put their feet upon the pedals, the wonderful bicycles began to move.

As they went along, ringing the little bells and laughing and chatting about such wonderful magical things, they found that they could make the bicycles go as fast or as slow as they wanted, by just wishing, "Go faster!" or "Go slower!"

It was lovely riding this way through the wonderful, mysterious woods and as they turned a bend in the path, they came to a tiny house, not a bit larger than a dog-house and it was almost hidden beneath large ferns.

"I wonder who lives in such a darling little house?" Raggedy Ann mused out loud as she brought her bicycle to a stop in front of the door.

"We shall soon see!" Raggedy Andy laughingly replied, knocking upon the door with his soft rag hand.

"Come in!" a little old man said as he held the little door open.

The Raggedys walked into the little house. "Why! Are you just moving in, or are you just moving out? There are no chairs to sit on!" Raggedy Andy said.

The little man looked very sad as he answered, "No! I am not just moving in, for I have lived here all the time, but I can't find a single chair growing in the woods on bushes, nor can I plant any chair seeds and get the seeds to grow into chair bushes! So I just have to sit upon the hard, hard floor all the time!"

10

"We have never heard of chairs growing upon bushes!" Raggedy Ann said, "but we have known of nice dresses and clothes and shoes and slippers growing upon MAGICAL bushes, because we wished for them ourselves."

"I do not care for new clothes," the little man said, "but it would be nice to have chairs so that my friends could sit on them when they visit me!"

Raggedy Andy whispered to Raggedy Ann, "Don't you remember, Raggedy Ann, you have a magic Wishing Pebble sewn up inside your cotton-stuffed body?"

"Why! I had forgotten all about it, Raggedy Andy!" Raggedy Ann replied. "I shall wish for a lot of nice little chairs for the little man!" And as soon as she wished for them, there stood the little chairs. The little man was so pleased he went out into his little garden and picked sixteen red lollipops for the Raggedys to eat during their visit. Then Raggedy Ann wished for some fruit cake and ice-cream and chocolate and butter-scotch, and they sat in the little chairs and rocked as they enjoyed the goodies.

Neepy—that was the little man's name—was very glad the Raggedys had come to see him. As they sat and talked with Neepy, there came a loud thump upon Neepy's little front door.

The thump was so loud, Neepy jumped right out of his chair.

"I smell goodies!" a gruff voice outside said. "Open the door so that I can come in and have some!"

"Dear me!" Raggedy Ann said, "Who can that rude person be, Neepy?"

Before Neepy could reply, there was another loud thump and a push and the little door flew open and in walked Gruffy Bear. "I smell goodies!" he said as he looked at the crumbs of the fruit cake and at the empty dishes in which the Raggedys and Neepy had had ice-cream.

"Why, Mister Gruffy Bear," Neepy said, "we have just finished eating all the goodies and there isn't anything left!"

"I'll just snoop in the cupboard and see!" Gruffy Bear said. "I'm sure you have some more fruit cake hidden!" And Gruffy Bear snooped in Neepy's cupboard.

"I can't find even a smidgin!" Gruffy Bear howled, "and the more I snoop around the hungrier I get for fruit cake! If you do not tell me where you have hidden it, I shall huff and puff and blow the roof right off this little house! That's what I shall do!"

"Honest, Mister Gruffy Bear," Neepy said, "all the fruit cake and ice-cream and the chocolate and the butter-scotch have been eaten up!"

"What?" Gruffy Bear howled, "You had ice-cream and chocolate and butter-scotch, the nice things I like, and you didn't save me any?"

"I am sorry, Mister Gruffy Bear," little Neepy said, "but how were we to know that you were coming? We just ate everything because everything was so good."

"That is just what makes me so angry!" Gruffy Bear howled. "So now I guess maybe I'd better eat you up first, then I'll eat your two friends up next!" And he pointed to Raggedy Ann and Raggedy Andy.

"No sir!" Raggedy Ann said. "You shan't eat anyone up!"

"Yes, I shall!" Gruffy Bear shouted. "I shall eat Mister Neepy first! Do you want me to start at your feet, or at the top of your head?" he asked little Neepy.

"I tell you where you can start!" Raggedy Andy said, as he gave Gruffy Bear a push which sent him rolling out of Neepy's little house, "you can start eating grass, or bushes, for you shan't even nibble little Neepy!" Then Raggedy Andy slammed the door shut and locked it before old Gruffy Bear could get upon his feet. "Now!" said Raggedy Andy, "let's have some more goodies just for fun and we will teach Gruffy a lesson for being so rude!" And so they all had lots more ice-cream and cake and other nice things.

"Oooh!" Gruffy Bear cried when he got to his feet and came back to the door, "I smell goodies plainer than I did before! I must have some! Open the door or I shall open it myself!"

"I have locked the door, old Mister Gruffy Bear!" Raggedy Andy said, "and now we are having ice-cream and cake all over again to teach you not to be so rude! People who ask for things nicely always receive them, but people who are rude and ill-mannered never get nice things!"

Gruffy Bear sniffed at the crack in the door, "Oooh!" he said, "I can smell the fruit cake as plain as anything! You'd better hurry and open the door before I huff and puff and blow the door in!"

"Maybe we had better open the door before he really huffs and puffs and blows it in!" little Neepy said as he looked from Ann to Andy.

"No sir!" Raggedy Andy laughed. "Do not let old Mister Gruffy Bear fool you that way, Mister Neepy! Gruffy Bear has read a story about the three little pigs and he can't huff and puff the door in at all!"

"If you don't hurry and unlock the door, I'll show you!" Gruffy Bear howled. "I can smell the fruit cake and ice-cream so plain it makes me want it more than ever! I'll count three and then I'll start and huff and puff!"

"Don't pay any attention to him!" Raggedy Ann told little Neepy, "and he will get tired and go away after a while!"

"Now I shall start!" Gruffy Bear howled, "ONE, TWO, THREE!" and he huffed as loud as he could, then he puffed as loud as he could.

13

"He makes the door rattle!" little Neepy said. "Shall I open it?"

Mercy! how Gruffy Bear huffed and puffed! He really could huff and puff a lot louder than the wolf huffed and puffed in The-Three-Little-Pigs story and the door rattled and shook. Then Gruffy Bear, seeing that he could not huff and puff the door in, got back and jumped with all his might at the door, and with a loud crash, the door came down and Gruffy Bear rolled into Neepy's little house. "Now give me the fruit cake and ice-cream, or I shall eat all of you up!" he cried as he got upon his feet.

But the Raggedys only laughed, because there wasn't any cake left except a few little crumbs and there wasn't any ice-cream at all. "Ha!" Gruffy Bear cried, "I shall eat you up first!" And he caught Raggedy Andy. But Raggedy Andy wasn't so easily fooled as Gruffy Bear thought, for as soon as Gruffy caught Andy, Andy caught Gruffy and they wrestled and wrestled until Raggedy Andy wrestled old Mister Gruffy Bear right out of the house and pushed him "Splash!" right into the brook. "Whee!" little Neepy and Raggedy Ann cried. "Raggedy Andy was the best wrestler! So now we will have some cream puffs!"

So Raggedy Ann wished for some cream puffs and they sat upon the grass to eat them.

Old Mister Gruffy Bear was all wet and soppy when he climbed out of the brook and he came over near the Raggedys and little Neepy and shook himself.

"Here!" Raggedy Ann cried, "don't shake yourself around here! You shake water all over us!"

"That's just what I wanted to do!" Gruffy Bear said. "I see you are eating cream puffs and I want some!"

"I should think when Raggedy Andy wrestled you into the brook that it would teach you not to bother us any more!" Raggedy Ann said.

"Ha, ha, ha!" Old Mister Gruffy Bear laughed. "The only reason Raggedy Andy could wrestle me was because I let him! that's what!"

"Of course, you let him!" Raggedy Ann replied. "Because why? Because you could not help letting him! Raggedy Andy is a lot better wrestler than you are!'

"Don't you believe it!" Old Mister Gruffy Bear said. "I was all tired from huffing and puffing at Mister Neepy's door! And as soon as I get rested and eat six, or seven of your cream puffs, then we will wrestle again and I will throw Raggedy Andy into the brook! Then I will throw little Neepy into the brook, then I will throw Raggedy Ann into the brook, then I will throw Neepy's little house into the brook and then I will throw—no!" Gruffy Bear corrected himself, "I won't throw anything else in the brook! Just all of you and the house! Now give me the cream puffs! Every one of them!"

"You shan't have a single one, Mister Gruffy Bear!" Raggedy Ann said, "not until you learn how to ask for them, nice and polite!"

"Then I will take them away from you!" shouted Gruffy Bear, as he started to grab the cream puffs from Raggedy Ann.

"Wait a minute!" Raggedy Andy said.

"Why should I wait?" Gruffy Bear howled. "Can't you

see I am getting hungrier and hungrier and hungrier every minute? And the hungrier I get, the angrier I get and in a few minutes I shall get so angry, I am afraid I shall eat you all up!"

"We will have to wrestle again, I guess!" Raggedy Andy said, as he rolled up his sleeves. "And I guess I will have to wrestle you into the brook again!"

"I don't want to wrestle again!" Old Mister Gruffy Bear shouted. "I told you that I was getting angrier and angrier! You don't want me to eat you up, do you?" But Raggedy Andy didn't answer Gruffy Bear again; instead, Raggedy Andy wrestled Gruffy Bear right down to the brook and pushed him in again.

"Now let's run and hide from him, so he can't find us!" Raggedy Ann suggested.

CHAPTER TWO

GRUFFY BEAR

SO while Old Mister Gruffy Bear was climbing up the bank, his clothes all wet and soppy, the Raggedys and little Neepy ran through the woods and hunted for a nice place to hide.

"Oh! I just thought of a place!" little Neepy said. "Do you Raggedys know where the Strawberry-flavoured Spring is?"

"No, where is it, Mister Neepy?" Raggedy Ann asked. "We have heard of lemonade springs and soda-water fountains, but we have never heard of a strawberry-flavoured spring! Have we, Raggedy Andy?"

"No!" Raggedy Andy replied, as he ran along beside Raggedy Ann and little Neepy.

"Do you know where the candy-covered cookie bushes grow?" little Neepy asked.

And when the Raggedys said they did not, little Neepy said, "Well then, I shall have to show you, for the Strawberry-flavoured Spring is right under the candy-covered cookie bushes, and as you sit and drink the strawberry-flavoured soda-water, you can reach right up and pick the candy-covered cookies and eat them!"

Little Neepy ran through the bushes and under logs until he came to a thick part of the deep, deep woods, and the Raggedys ran with him.

Sure enough, there they found the bushes of candy-covered cookies.

They crept in under the low branches of the cookie bush and there was the little Strawberry-flavoured Spring.

The Strawberry-flavoured Spring was as cold as ice— in fact, it was so cold that there were icicles all around on the grass at the edge.

The leaves of the cookie bush were shaped just like little drinking cups you see in the shops and all the Raggedys and little Neepy had to do, was to reach up and pick a cup and dip it into the Strawberry-flavoured Spring, then reach up and pick the candy-covered cookies and sit there and enjoy themselves.

I wish that everyone could have a strawberry-flavoured spring in his backyard and that there was a lovely cookie bush growing right over it.

"It all tastes so good, I wish Old Mister Gruffy Bear could have some, too!" little Neepy said. "Maybe the reason he is so ill-mannered is because no one has taught him to behave himself!"

"If Old Mister Gruffy Bear would be a nice Bear, it would be a pleasure for us to have him share the candy-covered cookies with us!" said Raggedy Ann.

"You two wait here, and I will run back through the woods and try and find Gruffy Bear!" said Raggedy Andy.

"All right!" Raggedy Ann and little Neepy said. "We will not eat any more candy-covered cookies, nor drink from the Strawberry-flavoured Spring until you return with Gruffy Bear."

So Raggedy Andy ran back through the woods to little Neepy's tiny house.

And when he got there, he heard loud voices. One was Old Mister Gruffy Bear's voice and he said, "Don't you dare take those two little shiny red bicycles!!'

"I will if I want to!" the other voice said and Raggedy Andy saw that it was a Snoopwiggy. "I found the little shiny red bicycles here and they are not yours, so I will take both of them. I need two bicycles to ride upon because I have four legs!"

"It doesn't make any difference if you have six legs!" Old Mister Gruffy Bear said. "Those two little shiny red bicycles belong to Raggedy Ann and Raggedy Andy, and if you take them, Raggedy Andy will wrestle you and throw you into the brook!"

"Pooh!" the Snoopwiggy replied. "Who's afraid to wrestle with Raggedy Andy, I'd like to know? He can't wrestle even a speck, I'll bet!"

"Ha! is that so!" Old Mister Gruffy Bear cried. "He can wrestle better than I can, for he threw me into the brook twice! And I'll bet I can wrestle you as easy as pie!"

"Huh!" the Snoopwiggy cried, real loud, "If you want to wrestle, I'll soon wrestle you into the brook for the third time!" And the Snoopwiggy ran at Mister Gruffy Bear and Old Mister Gruffy Bear ran at the Snoopwiggy and they hit together, "Blump!" The Snoopwiggy was a good wrestler for he had four legs and two arms, but that didn't keep Old Mister Gruffy Bear from throwing him right into the brook with a splash. "Now you can see who is the best wrestler!" Gruffy Bear laughed, "and I shall take the bicycles to the Raggedys so you can't have them!"

"I can catch you!" the Snoopwiggy said. "Just you wait!" But Raggedy Andy and Mr. Bear jumped on the bicycles and rode away leaving the Snoopwiggy to get out as best he could.

"You wrestled him fine!" Raggedy Andy told Mister Gruffy Bear. "I watched you all the time!"

"I wasn't going to let the Snoopwiggy take your two little shiny red bicycles!" Old Mister Bear laughed; "that's why I wrestled him!"

"I know it!" Raggedy Andy replied. "But what I can't understand is why you thought it was wrong for the Snoopwiggy to take our little bicycles, but you didn't think it

was wrong for you to try and take cream puffs away from Raggedy Ann?"

"Well, don't you see, Raggedy Andy," Gruffy Bear laughed, "when you threw me into the brook, two times, it washed me all off nice and clean!"

"Yes sir! You are a whole lot cleaner!" Raggedy Andy agreed.

"And that is just it!" Mister Bear said; "the water washed away every speck of Gruffiness and Grumpiness!"

"Oh goody!" Raggedy Andy said, "Raggedy Ann and little Neepy will be very glad! I came to take you to the strawberry-flavoured ice-cold Spring, where the candy-covered cookies grow!"

"Whee!" old Mister Bear cried with happiness, "that's just what I like best! Candy-covered cookies and ice-cold strawberry-flavoured soda-water!"

"And we will never call you Gruffy Bear again!" promised Raggedy Andy.

"How would it sound for you to call me Grinny Bear instead of Gruffy Bear? You see my initials begin with a G, so I must have a name which begins with the same letter!"

"I believe Grinny Bear will be a pleasant name, Gruffy Bear!" said Raggedy Andy.

"Now you see here!" Grinny Bear laughed, "just you call me Grinny Bear, Raggedy Andy, and leave off the Gruffy, because I don't care to be gruff or grumpy any more! It makes you feel inside all the time just like it was going to rain, or snow, or something, but since I am not gruff and grumpy, it makes me feel inside, just like a nice sunny day, with the birds singing and everything cheery and happy! It's a whole lot more fun than being gruff and grumpy!"

"I know it is, Grinny Bear!" Raggedy Andy laughed. "And I hope you never, never are disagreeable or ill-mannered again!"

"So do I!" Grinny Bear laughed. "Indeed, I shan't let myself get grumpy! If I feel the grumpiness coming on, I shall run and jump in the brook! That's what I shall do, Raggedy Andy!"

"You won't have to do that to get rid of the grumps and gruffiness!" laughed Raggedy Andy. "All you have to do, is just give your heart a 'sunshine bath' by saying, 'I love everyone!' "

CHAPTER THREE

THE SNOOPWIGGY AND THE WIGGYSNOOP

"IT'S a lot more fun being cheerful and kind than it is being gruff and grumpy!" Old Mister Grinny Bear said to the Raggedys and little Neepy as he came to where the Strawberry-flavoured Spring bubbled up from the ground beneath the candy-covered cookie bushes.

"Of course it is, Grinny Bear!" Raggedy Ann laughed as she handed Grinny Bear a leaf-cup full of Strawberry-flavoured Spring water. "Why do you ever doubt it?"

"Oh! I shan't any more!" Grinny Bear replied. "But before Raggedy Andy wrestled me into the brook, I was always grumpy and cross and gruffy! That is why everyone used to call me Gruffy Bear! But since Raggedy Andy threw me into the brook, I have felt so different it has been just like the golden sun peeping out after a black cloud passes by; that's how I have felt inside!"

"I guess it must have been a magic brook and that it washed away all your gruffy-grumps!" little Neepy said.

"No, it wasn't a magic brook!" a loud voice cried from the bushes, and here came the Snoopwiggy towards them.

"Oh, dear me!" Grinny Bear said. "Here comes the Snoopwiggy! I was hoping when I wrestled him into the brook, as Raggedy Andy wrestled me, that it would change Snoopwiggy as it changed me!"

"Well, it didn't!" the Snoopwiggy said, crossly. "And I am just as peevish as I was before. Now I shall chase all of you away from here, for I see these are candy-

covered cookie bushes! And that water from the Spring must be good, because you are not drinking it like water! You are drinking it like soda water, that's what! So you must all go away, or else I will start and chase you away! Then I will build a house right here and keep the candy-covered cookie bushes and the Spring all for myself!"

"We were here first, Mister Snoopwiggy!" Raggedy Ann said.

"What difference does that make?" the Snoopwiggy howled. "I want everything here all for my own, so you had better go before I begin chasing you away!"

"We shall stay right here, just as long as we want to!" Raggedy Andy said.

"I'll bet a penny, if I once start chasing you, then you'll go in a hurry!" the Snoopwiggy cried.

Raggedy Ann handed Grinny Bear and Raggedy Andy and little Neepy more of the Strawberry-flavoured Spring water, but she didn't ask the Snoopwiggy to have any. "Now!" the Snoopwiggy cried, "just because you are taking some more of that Spring when I told you I wanted it all myself, I shall begin to chase you away!" But as none of our friends started to run, the Snoopwiggy scratched his head. "I guess I will begin chasing little Neepy first, then Raggedy Ann, then Raggedy Andy, then Old Mister Gruffy Bear!"

"Don't you ever, ever call me Gruffy Bear again!" Grinny Bear cried as he jumped up, "because I am not Gruffy any more, so now I shall wrestle you again!" The Snoopwiggy did not wish to wrestle again, but Grinny Bear just made him, and he wrestled the Snoopwiggy so hard, that in a few minutes, Grinny made the Snoopwiggy run.

Raggedy Ann and Raggedy Andy laughed to see Grinny Bear chase away the Snoopwiggy. The Snoopwiggy was a very selfish creature, for instead of being kind and generous, he wanted the Strawberry-flavoured Spring and the candy-covered cookie bushes all for himself.

"Whee!" Grinny Bear laughed when he came back to the Strawberry-flavoured Spring, "did you see me chase away the Snoopwiggy? I'll bet he won't come back again!"

"We hope that if he does come back, he will be a better Snoopwiggy than he was before!" said Raggedy Ann. "The Strawberry-flavoured Spring and the candy-covered cookie bushes are plenty large enough for everyone, almost, in the deep, deep woods, so no one should be selfish with them. They belong to everyone in the deep, deep, deep woods!"

"Well! Here I am again!" the Snoopwiggy cried, as he came through the bushes, and, with a stick, knocked lots and lots of candy-covered cookies down upon the ground. "And I brought my friend, the Wiggysnoop, with me so that you can't chase me away again. The Wiggysnoop and I shall chase you away, now!"

"Don't you believe it!" Raggedy Ann said. "And besides, it is wrong for you to knock the candy-covered cookies off of the cookie bushes and waste them!"

"I don't care!" the Snoopwiggy cried as he started to knock more candy-covered cookies down from the bushes. "If the Wiggysnoop and I can't have some of the cookies, then we won't let anyone else have any and will chase everyone away from here!"

27

"I shall take a stick and stir up the Strawberry-flavoured Spring so that they can't drink any more from it!" the Wiggysnoop cried, picking up a stick and running towards the Spring.

"Now see here, Mister Wiggysnoop!" Raggedy Andy cried as he stepped before the strange creature, "it is always wrong to spoil anyone else's pleasure, just because you do not wish to enjoy that pleasure yourself! So if you try to stir up the Spring, I shall have to wrestle you!"

"Ha, ha, ha!" the Wiggysnoop laughed very loud, "did you hear that, Mister Snoopwiggy? I'll bet he can't wrestle worth two pins!"

"Don't you believe it!" Grinny Bear said. "Raggedy Andy is almost the best wrestler there is, I'll bet!"

"Pooh!" the Wiggysnoop laughed, "I'll bet he can't wrestle me at all!" And he caught hold of Raggedy Andy's arm and almost tore Raggedy Andy's pretty shirt.

Then Raggedy Andy took the stick away from the Wiggysnoop and wrestled him so hard he made the Wiggysnoop promise never to be nasty again. Then he wrestled the Snoopwiggy and made him promise, too. Then Raggedy Ann give them each a drink of the Strawberry-flavoured Spring and a whole lot of cookies.

"Why!" the Snoopwiggy said, when he tasted the Strawberry-flavoured Spring water and the lovely cookies, "this is so good that it is no wonder you did not want the Wiggysnoop and me to have it all to ourselves!"

"Such nice things should always be shared with others!" Raggedy Ann laughed, "for you will find out, Mister Snoopwiggy and Mister Wiggysnoop, that if you share your pleasures with others, the pleasures will seem ever so much better to you; 'cause, every time you give to others and make them happy, you catch some of their happiness, and that makes you just that much happier yourself! And the more you give away, the more you have yourself!"

"We have never tried that! Have we?" the Snoopwiggy asked the Wiggysnoop. "No!" the Wiggysnoop replied. "We always thought that the more you keep for yourself, the more you have! So we never have given anything to anyone else, and if we had a chance, we always took good things away from others!"

"My! My!" Raggedy Ann said, "of course that was being very, very stingy! And when one is stingy, it is just like shutting every door and window in a house and expecting the sunshine to come in! If you want to get real fun out of anything, just you try sharing it with another, then you'll see!"

"Do the Strawberry-flavoured Spring and the candy-covered cookie bushes belong to anyone?" the Snoopwiggy asked.

"I guess they belong to everyone in the deep, deep woods!" Raggedy Ann replied.

"But if they belong to everyone in the deep woods, how does it come that all the creatures are not here enjoying them?" the Wiggysnoop asked.

"I do not know!" Raggedy Ann replied. "Maybe the Strawberry-flavoured Spring and the candy-covered cookie bushes have not been here very long and not many people know of them!"

"Maybe!" the Wiggysnoop said.

"I tell you what let's do!" the Snoopwiggy said. "The cookies and the Strawberry-flavoured Spring water taste so good, we should let everyone in the deep, deep woods know about them! So the Wiggysnoop and I will run home and get my horn and the Wiggysnoop's drum, and we will have a parade and tell everyone about the place, and invite them here!"

So the Wiggysnoop and the Snoopwiggy ran home and soon returned with the drum and horn. Then, with the Wiggysnoop and the Snoopwiggy in the lead, Raggedy Ann and Raggedy Andy and Grinny Bear and little Neepy had a parade.

CHAPTER FOUR

THE BANG GUN

IT WAS a very nice parade that the Snoopwiggy and the Wiggysnoop and the Raggedys and Grinny Bear and little Neepy had through the deep, deep woods. The Wiggysnoop had a horn and the Snoopwiggy had a drum and they made lots of noise so that the little creatures all ran out to see what it was.

"Is there a circus in the deep, deep woods somewhere, Raggedy Ann?" the little creatures asked.

"Oh, no! There isn't a circus," Raggedy Ann answered, "but there is a very, very nice surprise waiting for you down beneath the candy-covered cookie bushes! Just run down this path and take the first left-hand turn to the right and you will come to the candy-covered cookie bushes."

And the more little creatures our friends sent to enjoy the goodies, the more laughter and happy chatter the Raggedys and their friends could hear as they went along, for the little creatures enjoyed the candy-covered cookies and the Strawberry-flavoured Spring soda-water so much that they danced and laughed, and they had so much fun it was just like a great big picnic party. Still the Raggedys and little Neepy and the Snoopwiggy and the Wiggysnoop and Grinny Bear marched along, telling more little creatures how to find the lovely cookies and the spring. Then, all of a sudden, they heard a real loud "BANG!" and the laughter and the chatter of the little creatures ceased as they raced in all directions.

"What was that?" Raggedy Ann said.

"I'll bet a penny it was a bang gun!" the Snoopwiggy said. "Let's all run and see who made the loud 'Bang!'"

So the Raggedys and the Snoopwiggy and the Wiggysnoop and little Neepy and Grinny Bear ran towards the Strawberry-flavoured Spring. And peeping through the bushes they saw a great big fat man and in his hand he held a long gun.

"Hmm!" Raggedy Ann said as she and her friends stopped, "What shall we do?"

"I tell you what let's do!" the Snoopwiggy said. "This man has never seen a Wiggysnoop, or a Snoopwiggy, I'll bet, so the Wiggysnoop and I will chase him away!"

"What if he shoots you with the bang gun?" Raggedy Ann asked.

"Ha, ha, ha!" The Snoopwiggy and the Wiggysnoop laughed, quietly. "You just watch!"

So the Snoopwiggy and the Wiggysnoop slipped quietly through the bushes until they were right behind the man. Then they jumped out and howled as loudly as they could. Grinny Bear and the Raggedys laughed and laughed to see how the fat man ran away.

"What did I tell you?" laughed the Snoopwiggy as he started blowing his horn and the Wiggysnoop started drumming.

And soon all the little creatures came back to the Strawberry-flavoured Spring and the candy-covered cookie bushes to spend the rest of the day enjoying themselves. "For," said Raggedy Andy, "the fat man was so surprised to see a Snoopwiggy and a Wiggysnoop, he will never come back, even to get the gun he dropped."

It was no wonder the fat man with the long bang gun ran, when the Wiggysnoop and the Snoopwiggy ran out in front of him and howled, for the Snoopwiggy and the Wiggysnoop were queer-looking creatures. And my! How they can howl when they want to.

Of course the Wiggysnoop and the Snoopwiggy mixed laughter into their howls, for the fat man was so frightened, when he saw the two strange creatures jump out in front of him, he rolled over and over many times before he got upon his feet and started to run.

"It served him right!" all the little woodland creatures said, when the Raggedys told them how the Wiggysnoop and the Snoopwiggy had frightened the fat man with the bang gun. " 'Cause why? 'Cause! That fat man comes into the deep, deep woods ever so often and when his gun goes 'Bang!' then nearly every time some little woodland creature gets hurt!"

"I do not see why some men like to do that!" Raggedy Ann said.

"Neither do I!" Grinny Bear said, "but they do!"

"Everyone with a bang gun that we see in the deep, deep woods, we will jump out and howl at! Won't we, Wiggysnoop?" the Snoopwiggy said.

"Indeed we will!" the Wiggysnoop replied. "I'll bet, if the Snoopwiggy and I had not been laughing so hard, we would have frightened him more than we did, for we can howl ever so much louder if we wish!"

"Maybe sometime we will ask you to howl real, real loud for us!" Raggedy Ann laughed, for the Wiggysnoop acted as if he wished to howl to show how loud he could howl, "But please do not howl now, because all the little woodland creatures are having so much fun, it might frighten them."

"All right!" the Wiggysnoop agreed. "We won't howl now!"

Just then Freddy Fox, who had run away when the fat man had shot the bang gun before, came running back to the Strawberry-flavoured Spring as fast as he could run. Freddy Fox was almost out of breath, but he said, "Do you know what, Raggedy Ann and Raggedy Andy?"

"What is it?" the Raggedys asked.

"Why!" said Freddy Fox, "I was hiding under a log

when I heard voices, and it was the fat man and another
fat man, and they said they were coming back here to get
the fat man's bang gun. You'd all better run!"

"Maybe we had all better hide!" Raggedy Ann suggested. So all the little woodland creatures ran and hid
beneath logs and in hollow trees and beneath stones. All
except the Snoopwiggy and the Wiggysnoop. They hid in
under the candy-covered cookie bushes and waited for the
two fat men. At first, the fat men did not think anyone was
near the Strawberry-flavoured Spring, but as soon as they
walked up beside the Spring, the Snoopwiggy and the Wig-

gysnoop both jumped out, one in front of each fat man, and
started to howl. My! How they did howl! Very much
louder than they had howled before.

"Mercy!" cried the fat man who had been there first,
"I never heard such loud howls! It makes my ears ache!
I don't believe I want to get my bang gun!" And he and
the other fat man ran away with their hands over their ears,
and never, never came back into the deep, deep woods to
bother the little creatures again.

When Raggedy Ann and Raggedy Andy left the happy
little woodland creatures drinking strawberry-flavoured soda-

water from the Spring which bubbled from the ground beneath the candy-covered cookie bushes, they said to the Snoopwiggy and the Wiggysnoop, "Wiggysnoop and Snoopwiggy, we are so glad that you have changed from selfish creatures into nice kind-hearted creatures, we are going to give you our little magic bicycles. For the little red shiny magic bicycles run along ever so fast and you do not have to work your feet to make them go. We know you will have lots and lots of fun riding upon them."

The Wiggysnoop and the Snoopwiggy were very pleased to get the nice red shiny magical bicycles, but they said, "Thank you ever so much, Raggedy Ann and Raggedy Andy! But if you give us the two red shiny magical bicycles, won't that make Grinny Bear and little Neepy feel badly because they haven't bicycles, too?"

"No indeed, it won't," Grinny Bear and little Neepy said. "We think it is nice for the Wiggysnoop and the Snoopwiggy to have the bicycles! And we are very happy that the Raggedys have given them to you!"

"Oh!" Raggedy Ann hastened to say, when Grinny Bear stopped talking, "It was very kind of the Wiggysnoop and the Snoopwiggy to think of Grinny Bear and little Neepy. It just shows that they have changed very, very much from selfish creatures into kindly generous creatures. But we did not intend to forget Grinny Bear and little Neepy. No sir! We gave the Wiggysnoop and the Snoopwiggy the two bicycles, and then we intended giving Grinny Bear and little Neepy, shiny red, magical bicycles, too!"

"Oh! Raggedy Ann!" the Snoopwiggy said, "how can you give away four shiny, red magical bicycles, when you only have two to give away?"

"Well!" Raggedy Ann laughed, "of course you do not know that I have a magical Wishing Pebble; a nice white one sewed up in my cotton-stuffed body! It's a secret, and all I have to do is make a wish and the wish comes true, right away! Doesn't it, Raggedy Andy?"

"Indeed it does!" Raggedy Andy replied. "And Raggedy Ann has a lovely candy heart, too, with the words, 'I love you,' printed upon it!"

"Then that's the reason the Wishing Pebble, which Raggedy Ann has sewed up in her body, works so well!" said the Wiggysnoop.

"So Raggedy Ann has a magical Wishing Pebble sewed up in her cotton-stuffed body, has she?" a gruff voice asked, and there stood a real tall man with a black cloak and a peaked hat. "I must have that Wishing Pebble, that's what! So hand it over to me!"

"How can she hand it over to you, when it is sewed up in her cotton-stuffed body?" Raggedy Andy asked.

The tall man did not answer. Instead, he jumped to catch Raggedy Ann, intending to take the Wishing Pebble away from her, I guess. But my! Didn't he get fooled? For he had only made one jump towards Raggedy Ann, when the Snoopwiggy and the Wiggysnoop and Grinny Bear made three jumps at him. "We'll teach you to bother Raggedy Ann!" the three good friends cried, and they pushed the tall magician, for that is what he was, this way and that, until they came to the brook, and then, splash, right into the brook.

CHAPTER FIVE

HOKUS THE MAGICIAN

THE Snoopwiggy and the Wiggysnoop and Grinny Bear ran back to where they had left Raggedy Ann and Raggedy Andy and Little Neepy. "Hurry!" Raggedy Ann cried. "Old Mister Hokus, the Magician, is climbing from the water and, my, but he is hopping mad!"

"It serves him right!" the Wiggysnoop laughed. "We won't let him take your magical Wishing Pebble, Raggedy Ann!"

The Wiggysnoop and the Snoopwiggy saw when they ran up to the Raggedys, that Raggedy Ann had wished for four more magic bicycles, all nice shiny red ones with rubber tyres. "Quick!" Raggedy Andy cried. "Here he comes! Hop on a bicycle and follow us!" And the Raggedys jumped upon their magical bicycles and raced down the path in the deep, deep woods followed by Grinny Bear, Little Neepy and the Wiggysnoop.

Maybe you have never seen a Snoopwiggy, so I will draw a picture of one. You can plainly see that he is not the kind of creature to ride a bicycle. Maybe he could ride an old-fashioned "tandem bicycle," for a tandem bicycle is built to carry two people. And the Snoopwiggy having four legs, really needed a double bicycle.

If Raggedy Ann had only thought of this, then they would not have had such an exciting adventure as they had.

When the Snoopwiggy jumped upon the bicycle, only two of his legs had a place to ride and the other two just stood upon the ground and kept the magic bicycle from going even a smidgin.

The Snoopwiggy tried kicking his two back feet and finally made the bicycle go a little bit, but not fast enough. So, when old Mister Hokus, the magician, shook the water from his coat and ran after the Snoopwiggy, he had no trouble in catching him at all. "Ha, ha!" old Mister Hokus laughed. "So you thought you could get away from me, did you, Mister Snoopwiggy?"

And before the Snoopwiggy knew what had happened, old Mister Hokus pulled him from the magic bicycle and tied a string around his neck.

"It is a magic string and the Snoopwiggy can't pull away, no matter how hard he tries!" the Magician said.

Then old Mister Hokus jumped upon the Snoopwiggy's bicycle and rode home and the Snoopwiggy trotted along behind, for the Magician held on to the other end of the string. When old Mister Hokus reached home, he took the Snoopwiggy into his kitchen and tied him to the table leg. Then he tied an apron around the Snoopwiggy's waist and said, "Now then! I have always wanted a servant girl, so you can cook the meals and sweep the kitchen and brush

the crumbs away, just like Little Orphant Annie, but if you try to escape, then the magic string will pull you right back into the kitchen!"

"I don't believe that at all!" the Snoopwiggy said, as he ran out of the kitchen door, lickety-split. The Snoopwiggy ran out of the door and almost across the porch, then the string jerked him back into the kitchen so hard he almost upset the stove.

"See?" Old Mister Hokus laughed. "Now you've got to stay right here in the kitchen!"

Maybe if the Snoopwiggy had not changed from a nasty creature into a kindly creature, he would have been very cross when old Mister Hokus, the magician, tied him to the table leg with the magic string.

"After you set the table, you can get dinner ready!" old Mister Hokus said, and he walked into the other room and began reading the Sunday newspaper just as if everything was settled.

The poor Snoopwiggy didn't know what to do. He had never even fried eggs before, or made biscuits, but he knew he had to get the dinner some way or other because old Mister Hokus looked very hungry.

Magicians always look hungry, but the Snoopwiggy did not know this.

"Let's see!" the Snoopwiggy said to himself. "Maybe I had better fry him a dozen eggs and make some coffee!"

So he put the frying pan upon the stove and placed six eggs in it and a lot of butter. Then he took a spoon and rolled the eggs around in the frying pan. Finally one of the eggs grew hot and the shell broke right in two and the egg spilled into the frying pan. Then another and another did the same thing until every egg was broken.

"Dear me!" the Snoopwiggy said to himself, "maybe he will be angry when he finds I have broken the eggs, so I guess I will put these away and get some new ones!"

So the Snoopwiggy scraped all the eggs into the fire and got six new ones. But these all burst open, too.

"This will never do!" the Snoopwiggy said. "They make the shells much too thin!"

Finally, after he had hunted all around, he found six nice shiny eggs. The Snoopwiggy thumped them and they seemed a lot harder than the others. So the Snoopwiggy put these in the frying pan with a lot of butter and stirred them around a long time. These nice shiny eggs did not crack open like the others, for these were china eggs with which old Mister Hokus, the magician, April-fooled his hens.

When the Snoopwiggy thought the china eggs had cooked long enough, he put them in a saucer and put salt and pepper and sugar on them.

"Dinner's ready!" he called to the Magician.

Just as soon as the Magician saw the dinner the Snoop-. wiggy had cooked, he said, "My goodness, how do you expect me to eat that kind of dinner?"

The Snoopwiggy just shuffled his feet because he didn't know what to say.

"I'll go back and read my Sunday paper until you cook me something a lot better than glass eggs!"

"Dear me!" the Snoopwiggy said, as he sat down and crossed his four legs, "I wish he would magic a nice dinner, because he is going to be real, real hungry before I try to cook again." And leaning back against the wall, the Snoopwiggy was soon fast asleep.

When Raggedy Ann and Raggedy Andy and Grinny Bear and little Neepy and the Wiggysnoop jumped upon the magic bicycles which Raggedy Ann had wished for, the little shiny red bicycles carried them so fast, they did not look behind until they had gone a long, long way.

Then Raggedy Ann stopped and said, "Why, where is the Snoopwiggy. Didn't he get upon his magic bicycle?"

"I saw him jump upon his bicycle, just as I got upon mine," little Neepy replied. "But you know, Raggedy

41

Ann, the Snoopwiggy has four legs and maybe he cannot ride a two legged bicycle!"

"Oh! I never thought of that!" Raggedy Ann said. "We must ride back and I will wish for a four-legged bicycle for the Snoopwiggy!"

So they all got upon their little shiny red bicycles and rode back the way they came until they reached the brook.

"Here is where the Snoopwiggy and the Wiggysnoop threw the magician into the brook!" Raggedy Andy said. "And here are the tracks of the Snoopwiggy's bicycle! See! He tried to ride it, but his back feet dragged upon the ground!"

"And look!" the Wiggysnoop cried. "Here are the tracks of old Mister Hokus, the magician! I'll bet six and a half pennies, he captured the Snoopwiggy!"

"That is just what he has done!" Raggedy Ann said, "so we will follow the tracks and see where old Mister Hokus, the magician, has taken the Snoopwiggy. Who knows? Maybe he changed the Snoopwiggy into a pig, or something, with magic, when he reached his home!"

When Raggedy Ann and Raggedy Andy and Grinny

Bear and little Neepy and the Wiggysnoop reached the home of old Mister Hokus, the magician, they left their bicycles by the back gate and tiptoed up to where they could peep into the kitchen.

There they saw the Snoopwiggy, sitting on the floor fast asleep.

"Psst!" Raggedy Andy said. But the Snoopwiggy was snoring so loudly he could not hear Raggedy Andy. Then Raggedy Andy tiptoed into the kitchen and awakened the Snoopwiggy. "Quick!" Raggedy Andy whispered. "We have come to rescue you from old Mister Hokus, the magician! Let's run out of the kitchen door as fast as we can and escape!"

"All right!" the Snoopwiggy replied, as he caught hold of Raggedy Andy's hand and started to run.

But the Snoopwiggy had forgotten that old Mister Hokus, the magician, had tied a magic string to the Snoopwiggy's neck and to the table leg, so when they reached the edge of the kitchen porch, the magic string pulled the Snoop-wiggy back into the kitchen and upset a chair, and the Snoopwiggy kept hold of Raggedy Andy's hand and pulled him back into the kitchen, too.

"Aha!" the Magician cried as he ran out to see what had caused the racket. "So Raggedy Andy came to rescue you, did he? Well, well! Now Raggedy Andy is captured, too, for you will find that neither one of you can let go of the other's hand!"

When the Magician went into his parlour to finish read-ing the funny pages of the Sunday newspaper, Raggedy Ann and Grinny Bear and little Neepy and the Wiggysnoop tip-toed up on the back porch and peeped in the kitchen window. Then Raggedy Ann said, "We must think of some way to rescue Raggedy Andy and the Snoopwiggy!"

Grinny Bear and Raggedy Ann and Little Neepy and the Wiggysnoop all sat down upon the Magician's back step to try and think of a way to rescue the Snoopwiggy and Raggedy Andy.

They thought and they thought and they thought, until finally Grinny Bear said, "I know! I will run around to the Magician's front door and knock, then when he comes to the door I will cry, 'Boo!' so loud he will be frightened and run away!"

"Oh!" Raggedy Ann told Grinny Bear, "Just let me think a minute longer!"

After thinking a minute longer Raggedy Ann held her rag thumb over her mouth as a sign for all to be very quiet, then she tiptoed into the Magician's kitchen where the Snoopwiggy was fast asleep with the magic string tied around his neck and to the table leg.

Then Raggedy Ann took a knife from the kitchen table and cut the string from around the Snoopwiggy's neck. Just as she had finished doing this, old Mister Hokus, the magician, came in.

"What are you doing here in my kitchen?" he cried in a loud voice; so loud, he awakened the Snoopwiggy.

"I've come to rescue the Snoopwiggy, and Raggedy Andy, that's what!" Raggedy Ann said.

"Ha! Ha!" the Magician laughed out loud. "How can you rescue him when I have a magic string around his neck?"

"Because," Raggedy Ann replied, "the Snoopwiggy was asleep with his fingers crossed and I cut the string then. Everyone knows that magic doesn't work when you cross your fingers."

And of course the Magician knew it, too, so he said, as Raggedy Ann and Raggedy Andy led the Snoopwiggy away, "You have rescued the Snoopwiggy this time, but just you let me catch him again, and you never, never will rescue him."

But Raggedy Ann and Raggedy Andy just walked right away with the Snoopwiggy and left the Magician sitting in the kitchen biting his finger nails.

"What I would like to know is how you rescued me when old Mister Hokus, the magician, had me tied to the

45

table leg with a magic string, Raggedy Ann?" the Snoopwiggy asked.

"I just fooled old Mister Hokus, the magician!" Raggedy Ann laughed. "I pretended that if you had your fingers crossed, the magic wouldn't work, and because old
Mister Hokus believed it, why, you see, it didn't work and
so I just rescued you, easy as pie!"

"I'm very glad you did!" the Snoopwiggy said, "for I
am not a very good servant girl!"

"A servant girl?" little Neepy asked. "How can a Snoopwiggy be a servant girl, when he is a Snoopwiggy boy?"

"That's just what I would like to know!" the Snoopwiggy replied. "But the Magician said that he had always
wanted a servant girl to cook his dinners and brush the
crumbs away and shoo the chickens off the porch, like Little
Orphant Annie, and that he wanted me to be his servant
girl! I tried to fry some eggs in butter, but just as soon as
the eggs grew hot, the shells popped open and they spilled

into the frying pan, then when I found some real hard eggs
and cooked them in butter, Old Mister Hokus, the magician, wouldn't eat them because he said they were April-fool
glass eggs he used to fool his chickens with!"

Raggedy Ann and Raggedy Andy laughed heartily at
what the Snoopwiggy said, for, lots of times at home, they
had seen Marcella's Granma put glass eggs in the nests so
that the hens would lay more eggs to hatch into fluffy little
baby chickens. And they had laughed when the Snoopwiggy had told of frying the real eggs and of the shells pop-
ping open.

"The next time you play servant girl, Mister Snoopwiggy," said Raggedy Ann, "you must put the frying pan
upon the stove, then put the fat into it, then break the shells
of the eggs and drop the eggs into the frying pan!"

"If you do that," the Snoopwiggy laughed, "then I
don't see why it makes any difference if you just put the
whole egg in and let it pop open!"

"Just because!" Raggedy Ann explained, "When you
do that, then the shell gets mixed with the other part of the
egg and it isn't good to eat! No one eats the egg shells!"

"I wish I had known that!" the Snoopwiggy said, "for
old Mister Hokus looked ever and ever so hungry and I
felt sorry for him!"

"Oh! you did, did you?" the Magician howled, as he jumped from behind a tree and caught the Snoopwiggy. "Well then, you can just come back home with me again and fry the eggs!"

The Wiggysnoop and Grinny Bear wanted to wrestle old Mister Hokus, the magician, and take the Snoopwiggy away from him, but the Magician crossed his fingers and said, "If it was fair for Raggedy Ann to rescue him when he had his fingers crossed, then it is fair for me to capture him again, when he doesn't have them crossed!"

And of course Raggedy Ann and Raggedy Andy knew it was best to play fair.

"I wish that you had let me wrestle with old Mister Hokus, the magician!" Grinny Bear said to Raggedy Ann as they watched the Magician walk away with the Snoopwiggy. "I could wrestle him just as easy as pie, and I would have thrown him into the brook again and rescued the Snoopwiggy!"

"Well, but don't you see, Grinny Bear, when I rescued the Snoopwiggy from the Magician before, when he had the Snoopwiggy tied to the table leg in the kitchen, I told the Magician that the reason I could rescue him was because the Snoopwiggy had his fingers crossed. And of course, everyone knows when you have your fingers crossed, that means "can't touch". So, if it was fair for me to rescue the Snoopwiggy from the Magician when the Snoopwiggy had his fingers crossed, then it is fair for the Magician to capture the Snoopwiggy when the Snoopwiggy doesn't have his fingers crossed!"

"Yes, I know!" Grinny Bear admitted, "but just the same, the Magician should not capture the Snoopwiggy! It isn't any fun for the Snoopwiggy to be captured and made to cook eggs for the Magician!"

"I know what let's do!" Raggedy Andy suggested. "Let's follow old Mister Hokus and the Snoopwiggy to the Magician's home, and when he makes the Snoopwiggy cook the eggs, let Raggedy Ann wish that the eggs would pop open and burn the Magician on the nose, then while he howls we can rescue——"

"Why, Raggedy Andy!" Raggedy Ann said, "it wouldn't be nice to make a wish like that, because it would hurt the Magician to have his nose burned. It is such a long one!"

"Then," Raggedy Andy again suggested, "why not wish for something real nice for the Magician—something that will please him so much, he will forget all about wanting the Snoopwiggy to do the cooking for him?"

"Yes!" Raggedy Ann agreed. "That would be a much better way to work it! Now what shall I wish for?"

Raggedy Ann had to make the wish, because she had a magical Wishing Pebble sewed up inside her cotton-stuffed body and every time she made a wish it would come true, just like in fairy stories.

"Maybe old Mister Hokus would like a pair of roller skates!" the Wiggysnoop suggested. The Wiggysnoop was very fond of roller skating on cement pavements and that is why he made that suggestion.

"But the Magician said he wanted the Snoopwiggy to cook for him!" Grinny Bear said, "so the wish must be for something to eat!"

"I believe Grinny Bear is right!" Raggedy Ann said. "Suppose I wish for a lot of ice-cream cones and lollipops and chocolate candy and cookies and everything to be right on the table, waiting for the Magician when he gets home?"

"That will be lovely, Raggedy Ann!" the Wiggysnoop said. "And I hope the Magician asks us in to help him eat them!"

"Well," Raggedy Ann laughed, "then I will wish that, too!"

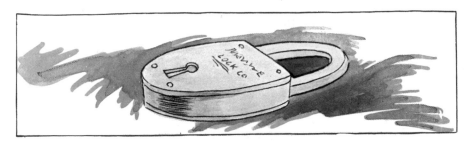

CHAPTER SIX

The Magic Lock

WHEN old Mister Hokus, the Magician, reached his home with the Snoopwiggy, he said, "Now I shall not let Raggedy Ann fool me again, as she did before! So instead of tying you to the table leg with a magic string, I shall put this magic lock in your pocket, then I will lock the lock and then I know you will not be able to run away for it won't make any difference even if you do cross your fingers, for this is a double spell and can't be broken with any amount of finger-crossing."

"Then I guess I shall never be able to escape!" the Snoopwiggy sadly sighed.

"I just guess you won't," the Magician promised. "I never yet found anyone who could escape when I put the magic lock in his pocket and locked the lock. Even if I have never tried it, I know he can't do it!"

Old Mister Hokus put the magic lock in the Snoopwiggy's pocket and locked the lock. "Now just you let me see you escape, Mister Snoopwiggy!" the Magician said.

"I shall not try!" the Snoopwiggy replied.

"It wouldn't do you even a speck of good to try!" the Magician laughed.

"Aw! I'll bet I could escape if I wanted to!" the Snoopwiggy said, as they walked into the Magician's house.

"Huh! I'll bet a penny you couldn't, even if you tried ever and ever so hard. Anyway, you must start right away and cook me something to eat, for I am getting hungrier

51

and hungrier every minute and the longer you put off cooking, the more you will have to cook!"

The Magician tied an apron around the Snoopwiggy and put a spoon in one of his hands and a frying pan in the other hand. "Now hurry!" he said.

The poor Snoopwiggy did not know what to do and was just about to sit down and try to go to sleep to forget all his troubles, when old Mister Hokus, who had gone into the dining-room, gave a glad cry and came running out. "You're the best hired girl I ever had!" he cried as he slapped the Snoopwiggy upon the back, "So take off your apron and come right into the dining-room and we will eat!"

The Snoopwiggy didn't know what to say, for he did not know that Raggedy Ann had made wishes for nice things to be on the Magician's table. So the Snoopwiggy just smiled and swallowed real hard and followed the Magician into the dining-room. There he saw the table piled high with goodies.

The Magician was just pulling up two chairs when Raggedy Ann and Grinny Bear and the Wiggysnoop and Raggedy Andy all knocked real hard on the door, THUMP! THUMP! THUMP! THUMP! like that.

"Ha!" the Magician cried as he ran to the door, "I hope that is company, because you cooked such good things and so many of them, I will have enough for six or seven people!"

And when he saw that it was Raggedy Ann and her friends, he cried, "Come right in and have dinner with the Snoopwiggy and me!"

And you see, that was just what Raggedy Ann had wished for, and it all came true, just like a fairy story. And, of course, all good things do really come true.

"Do you know!" the Magician said, as he pulled chairs up around his table for Raggedy Ann, Raggedy Andy, Grinny Bear, little Neepy, the Snoopwiggy, the Wiggysnoop and himself. "The Snoopwiggy is the best servant girl I ever had in my whole life, even if I never did really have a servant girl before! Why, I tied an apron around him and gave him a spoon and a frying pan and had hardly taken three steps until he had the table set and had cooked all the good things you see here!"

The Snoopwiggy chuckled as he passed the cream puffs to Raggedy Ann. "I expect, after all, Mister Hokus, Raggedy Ann must have fooled you again!"

"Ha, ha, ha!" the Magician laughed. "Don't you believe it, Mister Snoopwiggy! I have you fixed now so that you cannot escape! You see," he explained to the Snoopwiggy's friends, "I put a magic lock in the Snoopwiggy's pocket and I locked the lock—tick tock, like that—and he can't escape even if he wants to! So I know Raggedy Ann didn't fool me, for you are still captured!"

"Ho, ho, ho!" the Snoopwiggy laughed, as he passed the candy-covered cookies. "When you put the apron on me and handed me the spoon and the frying pan, I was just about to sit down and go to sleep, for I do not know how to cook anything; then you came running back and slapped me upon my back and told me the table was covered with goodies!"

"And you didn't cook any of these things?" the Magician asked in surprise.

"Not even one of the lollipops!" the Snoopwiggy replied. "Can't you see Raggedy Ann and Raggedy Andy and Grinny Bear and the Wiggysnoop and little Neepy giggling and smiling? They surely must have fooled you again, Mister Hokus!"

"Well! if Raggedy Ann fooled me again, I'd just like to know how she did it? 'Cause she wasn't even in the house after I captured you the last time!"

"I see that I shall have to tell you, Mister Hokus," Raggedy Ann laughed. "When you captured the Snoopwiggy, the second time, we didn't know how we could rescue him, so we thought and thought until someone thought that it would be nice to wish all these goodies right on your table, for we knew the Snoopwiggy did not even know how to cook beans! So I just wished for all these things and here they were! Then the Wiggysnoop wished that we would be asked to have dinner with you. I wished for that, too! And when we knocked upon the door, you asked us all into eat, and here we are."

"And it was very nice of you to ask us!" the Wiggysnoop said.

"We like you ever so much better now!" Grinny Bear said, "For by asking us in you showed that you are growing kinder and more unselfish!"

"I had not noticed it!" the Magician said, as he passed the Strawberry short-cake with the whipped cream over it. "How does it feel to be kinder, Raggedy Ann?"

"Well, sir!" Raggedy Ann softly said, "have you ever pushed the petals away from a white rose and looked at the yellow center? It looks just like sunshine! And when you open your heart to others, it is just like that and your heart seems to shine with sunny happiness!"

"I really do believe that I am growing kinder and more generous," old Mister Hokus, the magician, said, "for when I first captured the Snoopwiggy and told him I wanted him to be my hired girl, I know that if he had cooked me ever so good a meal I would never have asked anyone in to share it with me!"

"I guess you were very, very selfish then!" Raggedy Andy said.

"I guess I must have been!" the Magician agreed. "And do you know? While I was mean and selfish, noth-

ing ever seemed to go right with me! I was always bumping my head, or falling down and hurting my knees, or stubbing my toes when I went barefoot! And then, too, when I was selfish, it seemed just as if everyone wanted to harm me and as if they were trying to do things to make me peevish!"

Raggedy Ann and Raggedy Andy laughed and so did Grinny Bear and little Neepy and the Snoopwiggy and the Wiggysnoop.

"Why do you laugh?" the Magician asked them.

"I'll tell you!" the Snoopwiggy said. "When we first met Raggedy Ann, she and Raggedy Andy and Grinny Bear were having lots of fun. Now I had always been just like you before, but something happened—I guess it was a touch of Raggedy Ann's magical candy heart, or something. And instead of being peevish and selfish, I changed and became kind and happy! So that even when you were unkind to me, I didn't even bite you once, or howl at you!"

"I didn't know Snoopwiggys could bite!" the Magician said in a surprised tone. "And you were so quiet, I never even once thought you could howl!"

"I can howl beautifully!" the Snoopwiggy said. "But not as nice as the Wiggysnoop can howl!"

"He can howl a great deal better than I can howl!" the Wiggysnoop said, "only the Snoopwiggy is too polite to say so!"

"Don't you believe it!" the Snoopwiggy laughed.

"If I had known that, I never would have captured you!" the Magician told the Snoopwiggy, "for I would have been afraid that you might bite me, and I would run like the dickens if you howled!"

"I shan't howl then!" the Snoopwiggy laughed.

"I guess just to be on the safe side, I had better unlock the lock and take it out of your pocket! For I am afraid you might forget and howl even if you don't mean to!"

"Do you mean that you will uncapture me, yourself?" the Snoopwiggy asked.

"That's just what I mean!" the Magician laughed. "You see, I really can't make a servant girl out of you, anyway, because you are a boy Snoopwiggy, and anyway, I feel so happy inside, I cannot bear to think of you being unhappy!"

"Then you will make me very happy if you take the magic lock out of my pocket," the Snoopwiggy said. The Magician did this and then said, "Now I will tell you a secret! I am not even a teeny weeny speck of a magician! I was just pretending it all the time!"

"And the magic lock wasn't a lock at all?" the Snoopwiggy asked.

"Sure! It was a lock!" the Magician replied. "But it wasn't a magic lock! 'Cause why? 'Cause I bought it at the corner shop and anyone can buy as many as he wants, just like it, for ten cents!"

"Why not make a real magic lock out of it, just for fun?" Raggedy Ann said.

"How can we make it a magic lock, when it is only a corner shop lock?" Mister Hokus asked.

"Well," Raggedy Ann replied, "we can either pretend it is a magic lock, or I can wish it to be a real-for-sure magic lock. And, of course, if I wish it to be a real-for-sure one, then of course it will be. Because I have a Magic Wishing Pebble sewn up inside my cotton-stuffed body and every time I make a good wish it comes true!"

"Then do you mean me to put the lock in the Snoopwiggy's pocket and lock it so that he cannot escape? You do not mean that, do you, Raggedy Ann? 'Cause I do not wish to make the Snoopwiggy my servant girl to cook my meals when he doesn't know how to cook!"

"Oh, no!" Raggedy Ann laughed. "I meant that I would wish it to be a real-for-sure magic lock and we could all take turns putting the lock in our pockets; then when we lock the lock, the magic would make it lock up our friendship forever and ever!"

"Raggedy Ann!" Grinny Bear cried, "that is a lovely thing to do and we will all love you for doing it!"

"All right!" Raggedy Ann laughed happily. "Then I make the wish that the lock will be a real-for-sure magical lock, and that whenever Mister Hokus wishes to make a friend, all he will have to do will be to ask the person to put the lock in his pocket, then, Mr. Hokus, you can lock the lock and you and the person will be good friends forever. When you have many kindly thoughts, it makes your life ever so happy; for each thought the friend wishes, of course you wish him a kindly thought in return."

"Then if I have a real-for-sure magical lock, I will really be a magician, won't I?" the Magician asked.

"Indeed, you will!" Raggedy Ann replied. "And if you put the lock in our pockets, you will be a magician, right away!"

CHAPTER SEVEN
A Real Magician

RAGGEDY ANN could always think of the nicest things to wish for. Maybe it was because she had a candy heart with the words, "I love you," printed on it, and maybe it was just because she was stuffed with nice clean white cotton.

Raggedy Andy did not have a candy heart and, while he could not think of as many nice things, still he could think of quite a lot, and he was stuffed with nice clean white cotton, too.

So maybe it was because Raggedy Ann had both the candy heart and the nice clean white cotton stuffing, too, that she thought of the nicest things.

So Mister Hokus put the new magic lock in the Snoopwiggy's pocket and locked it, then in the Wiggysnoop's pocket and then in Grinny Bear's pocket and then in Little Neepy's pocket and then in Raggedy Andy's pocket and then in Raggedy Ann's apron pocket.

When old Mister Hokus put the lock in Raggedy Ann's pocket, he whispered to her, "I'm going to lock the lock two times so that we will always be two times good friends."

Raggedy Ann laughed as Mister Hokus locked the lock

two times and then she said, "Now I'll bet a penny, Mister Hokus, that you are two times as good at magic as you were before! Just you try to magic something and see!"

"Won't it be nice, if I really am a magician?" Old Mister Hokus cried. "I can think of a great many nice things to magic already! First, I believe I will see if I can magic some ice-cream cones, for it has been almost ten minutes since we had dinner, and I know you must all be getting hungry!"

So Mister Hokus rolled up a piece of paper into a cone, little at one end and large at the other. Then he rolled up his sleeves and said, "I just wish to show you that I have no ice-cream cones up my sleeves!"

Then he took a little stick and tapped the paper cone three times, because that is a very magic number and said, "Hokus-pokus!"

Then he shook the cone in front of Raggedy Ann and out fell a nice strawberry ice-cream cone. Then in front of Raggedy Andy, and he received a lemon ice-cream cone. The Snoopwiggy and the Wiggysnoop each received a chocolate ice-cream cone and Grinny Bear and little Neepy a pineapple ice-cream cone.

"It's working fine!" Old Mister Hokus laughed. "You surely made a fine magician out of me, Raggedy Ann, and I thank you ever and ever so much! Now I will show you something else! See how short my beard is? Well! Real for sure magicians should have long beards! At least, all the magicians in fairy stories do. So I shall grow myself a real long beard."

So old Mister Hokus wiggled his wand in front of his face and said, "Hokus-pokus!" three times, and immediately his short whiskers began growing. "Look!" he cried after a moment. "They have grown two inches already! Now I shall soon have nice long whiskers, like I have always wanted!"

"Don't let them get too long, Mister Hokus!" Little Neepy said. "If they grow too long, you will look like a Billy-goat!"

"Oho!" Mister Hokus laughed. "I do not wish to look like a Billy-goat, so I shall let them grow three feet long, then they will be a lot longer than any Billy-goat's whiskers and I shall look just like a fairy story magician and that is just what I want."

Old Mister Hokus was very proud of the way his whiskers grew, and he walked to the looking-glass, every minute, to see how nice they were.

Finally, when his whiskers had grown until they reached down to his knees when he stood up, Mister Hokus stood in front of the looking-glass and asked, "Now! Don't you think they are just right, friends?"

"They are just right, now!" Raggedy Ann and Andy and Grinny Bear and little Neepy and the Snoopwiggy and the Wiggysnoop agreed.

"I think so, too!" old Mister Hokus proudly said, "So now I shan't let them grow any longer!"

Then he waved his little wand in front of his face and said, "Hokus-pokus!" three times. Still his whiskers continued to grow.

In fact, it seemed to hurry the whiskers more than ever and they grew until they touched the floor.

"Dear me!" old Mister Hokus cried, "What shall I do? They are much too long!"

"Why not cut them off just where you want them?" Raggedy Andy asked.

"I hadn't thought of that!" Mister Hokus said with a relieved sigh.

But when he cut a foot and a half from the whiskers, just as soon as he cut, the whiskers grew three feet. Then Mister Hokus cut his whiskers off near his chin. Immediately the whiskers grew twice as long as they had been before. Upon seeing this, old Mister Hokus began crying

61

and everyone felt sorry for him. For now his whiskers were more than two times as long as Mister Hokus, so that when he started to walk to the looking-glass, he stepped upon his whiskers and fell down.

Maybe it is a lot of fun being a magician and making ice-cream cones appear right out of a paper cone, but it isn't any fun to be in a fix like old Mister Hokus found himself. The whiskers were so long, Mister Hokus could not walk at all and there was scarcely room in the house for the whiskers and Raggedy Ann and Raggedy Andy and Grinny Bear and Little Neepy and the Snoopwiggy and the Wiggysnoop.

"What, oh, what shall I do?" the Magician cried.

"The best thing to do is to put the scissors away!" Raggedy Ann advised. "For you just make the whiskers twice as long each time you cut them off!"

"I know it!" old Mister Hokus cried, as Raggedy Ann wiped his eyes with her apron. "But I wanted nice whiskers just like all fairy story magicians have and I had no idea the magic wouldn't work properly! Can't you try wishing the whiskers away, Raggedy Ann? I do not care now even if I don't have any whiskers at all!"

"I'll try!" Raggedy Ann said, as she sat down in a corner of the room by herself and held her hands over her eyes. You see she had shoe buttons for eyes, and, of course, no one with shoe buttons for eyes can close them and wish real hard like real boys and girls can do.

"Now please, everyone be real quiet!" Raggedy Andy said. "For Raggedy Ann wishes to wish harder than she ever wished before, I guess!"

Raggedy Ann wished and wished for old Mister Hokus to have whiskers only as long as he wanted them to be. But although Raggedy Ann ripped four stitches out of the back of her head, where they didn't show, the whiskers remained the same length, but they changed from grey whiskers to an emerald green.

"Oh, how lovely!" Raggedy Ann cried when she took her hands from her eyes.

"Oh dear, oh dear!" Mister Hokus howled. "They are worse than ever before. Something must be done!"

But as no one could think of anything to do, they just sat there and wondered and wondered.

And after looking at the magician's green whiskers for a time, whenever they looked at anything else, even if it was white, it looked like red. If you look at a piece of green paper for awhile and then look at a piece of white paper, you will see what our friends saw.

CHAPTER EIGHT

The Witch's Magic

RAGGEDY ANN and Raggedy Andy and Grinny Bear and little Neepy and the Snoopwiggy and the Wiggysnoop all felt very sorry for their friend, old Mister Hokus, the Magician.

"Dear me! I do not know what to do!" Raggedy Ann sighed. "I wished just as hard as I could, but I seem to have made things worse!"

"The only thing I know to tell you," Grinny Bear finally said, "is that, deep in the centre of the woods, there lives a Witch, and maybe if we go to her she can undo the Magician's magic!"

"Then we had better take poor Mister Hokus to the Witch at once!" Raggedy Andy said. "For pretty soon, if his whiskers continue to grow, they will be so long he will be unable to drag them through the woods."

"We had better start right now!" the Magician said, as he stood up and stepped upon his long whiskers and fell down again.

"I know what we will do!" the Snoopwiggy said. "I will take the first part of the Magician's whiskers and the Wiggysnoop the next part, and Grinny Bear the next part, and little Neepy the next part, and then Raggedy Andy the next, and then Raggedy Ann the next part. If we do not do that way, then someone will have to carry him!"

And that is the way they arranged it. They made a queer looking parade as they walked along and the Magician felt very sad.

They walked and walked until they came to the Witch's little tumble-down house, and the Snoopwiggy, who was in the lead, knocked upon the door.

The Witch peeped out a chink in the door and when she spied who it was, she said, "Go away from here!"

"But we came to get you to unmagic the Magician's whiskers," the Snoopwiggy said.

"I know you did!" the Witch howled in a loud shrieking voice. "I shan't unmagic my own magic! I made his whiskers grow longer and longer on purpose, because I do not wish anyone else in the woods to use magic except me!"

"Then you are very selfish and unkind!" Raggedy Ann spoke, "and I am sorry that we came to you! We thought you might be a nice friendly witch. Instead you are unkind and selfish!"

"Don't you say that I am selfish!" the old witch howled at Raggedy Ann out of the window, "I'll make all of you have real long whiskers! That's what I shall do!"

"Then you will be meaner than ever!" Grinny Bear said. "And if Raggedy Ann will let me, I will come right into your house and bite you harder than hard!"

"Oh you would, would you?" the Witch howled, when she heard what Grinny Bear said. "Just for that, I shall grow whiskers on all of you, so there!"

And before they had gone twenty feet, Grinny Bear and the Snoopwiggy and the Wiggysnoop and the Raggedys had whiskers on their chins.

The Raggedys had yarn whiskers and they looked very funny.

"Whee!" Raggedy Ann cried, "Look at my whiskers! Just what I have always wanted all my life!"

And the Snoopwiggy and the Wiggysnoop and Grinny

Bear and little **Neepy and Raggedy Andy** all cried, real loud, "Whee! Look at our fine, nice whiskers! That was just what we wanted all the time!" And they winked at one another.

Now when the mean old Witch heard them shouting as if they were greatly pleased at having the whiskers on their chins, this made her very angry, for she did not wish to please anyone if she could help it.

"Dear me! How careless of me! I should have known that they came here especially to get whiskers like old Mister Hokus! Now I shall have to take the whiskers away from them again!"

And before the Raggedys and their friends had gone very far, they felt the whiskers disappear from their chins, and they looked at one another and winked.

Then the Snoopwiggy whispered to the rest and said, "Maybe if old Mister Hokus cries, 'Whee! I've got the best whiskers in the world!' and pretends to be glad because we haven't any whiskers, the old Witch will take his whiskers away from him!"

So they all walked back to the Witch's tumble-down house and Mister Hokus kicked up his heels and cried, "Whee! I've got the best and the longest whiskers in the world! If my whiskers were only two feet long, I would be unhappy!"

"Ha! What is this I hear?" the old Witch whispered to herself. "I must have made a dreadful mistake. I shall make his whiskers only two feet long so that he will be unhappy!" And she did this in just a few moments.

"Oh dear!" Mister Hokus cried. "Now I shall be unhappy for my whiskers are only two feet long!" And for fear the old Witch would catch on to the way our friends had fooled her, they hurried away through the woods, howling loudly as if they really were very unhappy.

But as soon as they were out of the Witch's sight, they all caught hold of hands and danced joyously.

"That was the time we fooled the old Witch!" Mister Hokus laughed. "Now if my whiskers would only grow white again, instead of staying green, I would look just like a real for sure magician!"

"Maybe, now that your whiskers are just long enough, if you work your magic you can change the colour!" the Snoopwiggy suggested.

"Maybe I can!" the Magician said, "At least, I shall try it!"

So old Mister Hokus rolled up his sleeves to show that he did not have any colours up his sleeves, then he waved his little magic wand in front of his face and said, "Hokus, Pokus, I want my whiskers to be white instead of green! How do they look now?" he asked when he had finished working all the magic he knew.

"They are still as green as ever!" Raggedy Ann said.

"And they have started growing again!" Raggedy Andy cried. "They have grown at least a foot longer!"

"Oh dear!" the Magician cried. "I guess I should have let well enough alone!" And indeed, this is what he should have done, for his beard continued to grow and grow until it was ten feet long.

Tears came in the Magician's eyes and he would have cried, but Raggedy Ann hurried and wiped the tears away with her hanky—the one with the blue border. "It just goes to show that one should be satisfied when he has things fairly good!" the Magician sighed. "If I had not tried to improve on my whiskers, they would have been all right, for green is a nice colour and it isn't everyone who can have green whiskers!"

"No indeed!" Raggedy Andy agreed. "The only other person I ever heard of who had coloured whiskers was Blue Beard! And just see how well known he was!"

"It will do no good returning to the old Witch's house, will it?" the Magician asked.

"Maybe it might!" the Wiggysnoop said. "Maybe we can fool her again!"

"No, you can't," the Old Witch howled as she poked her head out from behind a tree. "I heard every word you have said, and I'll bet a penny that you will not fool me again!" And laughing softly to herself, she waddled away through the woods, towards her little tumble-down house.

"I don't care, anyhow!" the Magician laughed. "I can wrap my beard around my neck in the winter time and it will keep me nice and warm! And just to show the old Witch that it does not make me very unhappy, I shall make a lot of magic goodies and we will have a picnic right here where we are sitting!"

And the Magician said a few magic words, and there upon the ground in front of them, appeared a table-cloth and upon the table-cloth was everything nice to eat you could imagine. So Raggedy Ann tucked the Magician's beard round behind him and helped everyone to cream puffs, ice-cream cones and all the other goodies.

When they had almost finished eating, the Magician looked up and saw a little man standing over beside a tree looking at him.

"Hello, little man!" the Magician cried as he waved his hand to the little fellow. "Won't you come over and have some of our goodies?"

69

"Thank you very much!" the little man replied, as he came up to the magic table-cloth. "I was just wishing that I had something to eat!"

"Then you must sit down here with us and have everything you wish!" the Magician said, "And if there isn't enough, I shall make a whole lot more with my magic!"

"Oh! There will be plenty!" the little man replied as he sat down between Raggedy Ann and the Magician.

And indeed, there was plenty, for the Magician's magic worked fine except when he tried to change his whiskers. And the reason his magic did not work as well when he tried to change his whiskers, was because the old Witch's magic was stronger than his.

When the little man had finished eating as much as he wished, he asked the Magician if he had tried cutting off his whiskers.

"Oh, yes!" the Magician replied. "But whenever I cut any of them off, they grew just twice as long as they were before!"

"I see, then, that the mean old Witch has worked her magic on your whiskers!" the little fellow said. "But if

70

71

you will come over to my house, I believe I can cut off your whiskers so that they will be just as long as you wish them to be, and no longer!"

"Can you work magic?" Raggedy Andy asked the little man.

"Oh, no!" the little fellow replied. "If I could, I would not have been so hungry when I stood and watched you enjoying the goodies here! But I know that there is a way to fool the old Witch and if you will come to my house, I will try it!"

"Maybe if you cut off the Magician's whiskers, they will grow twice as long as they are now, and then they will be twenty feet long instead of ten!" the Snoopwiggy said.

"I do not believe so!" the little man said as he led the way through the woods towards his house.

"If you can get rid of the magic the Witch worked on my beard, I will make you a very nice present!" the Magician promised.

"Thank you very much!" the little man laughed. "But I do not expect payment for doing a kindness to another!"

"That is exactly how we should always feel!" Raggedy Ann said, "for, whenever we do a kindness to another, we always get much pleasure from doing it and that alone is payment enough!"

CHAPTER NINE

THE MAGICIAN'S LONG GREEN WHISKERS

WHEN Raggedy Ann and Raggedy Andy and the Magician and Grinny Bear and Little Neepy and the Snoopwiggy and the Wiggysnoop reached the little man's house in the deep, deep woods, they found a lovely little place.

Of course, the little man's house was a tiny little house, made just the right size for such a tiny little fellow as he. And the curved red roof looked very pretty against the green ferns and bushes.

The little house stood right at the side of a pretty little brook and the little man had built a little water-wheel which turned over and over as the water rushed against it. And from the little water-wheel to the little house there were lots of strings and the turning of the water-wheel made the strings turn over a lot of cute little toys.

"Just as soon as we get the Magician free from the Witch's magic, I will show you all the pretty little moving toys I have made!" the little man promised.

The little man brought a long rope out of his house and tied it to a limb of a tree.

Then he asked the magician to stand upon a ladder.

"I do not see why you want me to stand upon the ladder!" the Magician said.

"Just you wait a minute and you will see why!" the little man laughed.

Then he tied the rope to the Magician's whiskers.

When this was done, and the Magician stood upon the ladder, the little man brought out a large pair of shears. "Dear me!" the Magician cried, when he saw the little man with the shears, "don't you know that if you cut my whiskers off, they will grow just twice as long?"

The little man laughed and then replied, "Please do not worry! I believe that I can fool the old Witch's magic! Now here we go!" And he took the ladder out from under the Magician so that the Magician hung in the air with his whiskers tied to the rope.

The Magician kicked and wiggled around a little bit, for it felt funny to find the ladder taken away from under him, but the little man said, "Please do not wiggle and kick so hard, for I may snip your chin if you move about!"

Then he reached up with the large shears and with one snip he cut right through the long whiskers.

As soon as the whiskers were snipped in two, the Magician tumbled to the ground and sat there feeling the remaining part of his beard.

"Whee!" the Snoopwiggy and the Wiggysnoop and Grinny Bear and Little Neepy and the Raggedys cried. "Your whiskers are not growing a speck, Mister Hokus!"

"I really believe you have fooled the old Witch's magic!" the Magician said to the little man. "How in the world did you do it?"

The little man laughed again as he said, "Well sir! Before, when you tried to get rid of the magic whiskers, you cut the whiskers off of you! But I fooled the old Witch's magic! For, instead of cutting the whiskers from you, I cut you from the whiskers!"

And indeed, this was true, for, there hanging from the tree were the Magician's whiskers and they had grown twice as long as they had been before; but this did not bother the Magician now, for the long whiskers were not hanging upon his chin as they had been before.

Raggedy Ann and Raggedy Andy were very happy when the little man had finished cutting the Magician off of his long whiskers.

"It isn't very nice to have such long, long whiskers!" the Magician laughed, "and I am so grateful to the little man. I shall work him a nice magical present!"

"My goodness!" the little man laughed in reply, "I do not expect anything in return for what I did! It is always a pleasure for me to do a kindness to another, and I do not want you to pay me!"

"I know just how you feel!" the Magician said, "but, please remember this: if it makes you happy to do a kindness for another, don't forget that it makes me happy to do something nice for another, too. So I wish to make you a magical present; and, if the present makes you happy, then, of course, it will make me happy, too!"

"Indeed! It will make all of us happy, too!" Raggedy

Ann said. "So, little man, please let the Magician make you a magical present!"

"If it will make all of you happy to see me get a very magical present, then, of course, I shall be glad to let the Magician give me something. But if I may have a wish, then I shall wish that the present shall be something which all of us may share!"

"Now I know that my magic will work well!" the Magician laughed. "For whenever I make real unselfish magic, it always is very good magic! So if you will tell what you would like me to make, I will make it just as quickly as I can!"

"I don't know what to wish for!" the little man replied. "Sometimes I have thought if I had a whole lot of things to play upon, like roller coasters and merry-go-rounds and swings and chutes and all those things, that it would be very nice. For then, I could let all the people who enjoyed play= ing upon such things come right into my place and enjoy themselves!"

"Do you think you could make so many nice things, Mister Hokus?" Grinny Bear asked.

"I can try!" the Magician replied. "You see," he explained to the nice little man, "I have not been a Magi-cian very long! Raggedy Ann wished that I would be a Magician and her wish came true! But I do not know just how good my magic will work on real big things. So, first of all, I will magic some pop-corn and peanuts and lemon-ade; then, if I can magic the nice things you want, we can have the peanuts and pop-corn to eat, while we play upon the merry-go-round and other things."

So the Magician said "Hokus Pokus," and immedi-ately everyone had a packet of peanuts, pop-corn, and a bottle of lemonade. Then he said "Hokus Pokus," sixteen times, and there was a merry-go-round, the chute, the swings and all the other things you usually find in a plea-sure park.

So the Raggedys and the little man and the M..
and Grinny Bear and little Neepy and the Snoopwiggy
the Wiggysnoop took their goodies and played upon the
merry-go-round and the other things until all the little
creatures living nearby came and watched them. When
the little man saw this, he said, "Let's invite all the little
creatures to play, too!" And when they did this, the Magician made goodies enough for everyone who came to play.
So you can imagine just how much fun everyone had.

And, while the Raggedys and the Magician and all their
friends and the little woodland creatures were playing upon
the merry-go-round and other things, and were laughing
and shouting and having a lot of fun, Raggedy Ann looked
over towards some bushes and saw the old Witch standing
there watching them.

"Hmm!" Raggedy Ann said to herself, "I wonder if
the old Witch is trying to make the Magician's magic stop
working? For if she makes it stop working, all these nice
things will disappear and the little man and the little woodland creatures will not have a thing to play upon!"

So Raggedy Ann hopped from the merry-go-round and
ran over to where the old Witch stood. "Please, Missus
Witch," Raggedy Ann said, "do not unmagic the Magician's magic, for if you do, you will spoil everybody's
fun!"

The old Witch did not answer Raggedy Ann, because
she couldn't. Her eyes were filled with tears and there was
a lump in her throat.

Raggedy Ann took her nice clean hanky and wiped the
old Witch's eyes. "Now I'll bet you feel better! Don't
you?" she asked, as she put her rag arm around the old
Witch's shoulder.

"I heard all the laughing and fun going on, so I came
to see what it was!" the old Witch said. "And it made me
feel very, very sad, when I saw what nice things the Magician had made for all the woodland creatures, to think how

77

hard I tried to keep the Magician from working his magic. So I just stood here and cried and cried!"

"Well! Don't cry any more!" Raggedy Ann laughed. "Just you come along and hop on the merry-go-round and see how much fun it is!"

At first, the old Witch didn't want to do this, but Raggedy Ann took her arm and pulled her right over to the merry-go-round and found her a seat upon a shiny white horse.

"Whee!" the old Witch cried, when the music started and the merry-go-round went around and around. "No wonder everyone enjoyed it so much! This is the most fun I've ever had!" And she laughed and yelled, just as happily as anyone else.

Then Raggedy Ann took her to all the other things and she enjoyed them as much as she had the merry-go-round. "Do you know what?" she said to Raggedy Ann, "after this, I shall never use any kind of magic except to bring pleasure to someone else, 'cause just look at the nice Magician. You can see that he is getting as much fun out of these nice things as anyone else!"

"Indeed, Missus Witch, that is quite true," Raggedy Ann replied. "If you just try it, you will soon find out, that whenever you do something kindly for another, you plant a seed inside your own heart, which grows into a happiness blossom, and, for every speck of fun you give another, you receive an echo of that fun yourself!"

79

CHAPTER TEN

THE MAGICAL SAFETY PIN

RAGGEDY ANN knew what she was talking about when she told the old Witch that every time anyone did a kindness for another it planted a seed within the heart which soon grew into a happiness blossom.

The old Witch said to Raggedy Ann, "It makes me feel sad when I see the merry-go-round and the other things the Magician made for the woodland creatures to enjoy. It makes me feel ashamed to think of the way I tried to unmagic the Magician's magic. So I shall go over under that big tree and sit down and try to think of something nice to give to the Magician."

"Maybe I can help you think of some nice things, Missus Witch!" Raggedy Ann said. "If you would like me to go with you, I will, and maybe I can think of something nice to magic, too!"

"Can you magic, too?" the old Witch asked.

"Oh yes!" Raggedy Ann replied. "But I am not a witch, nor a magician. I have a real-for-sure Wishing Pebble sewn up inside my cotton-stuffed body and almost every time I make a wish, the wish comes true!"

"It must be very nice to own a Wishing Pebble!" the Witch said, as she put her arm around Raggedy Ann and they walked over to the large tree. "Please tell me how you happened to get the real-for-sure Wishing Pebble! I

have looked and looked and looked for a Wishing Pebble, but I never could find one!"

"I found this one by the laughing brook!" Raggedy Ann said, as she sat down beside the Witch, "and lots and lots of times I have had jealous persons try to take it away from me! But in the end, they all turned out to be nice, for, after they found out that there is always lots more fun in being kind and good than there is in being selfish and mean, they changed from mean to good. Then, of course, they did not wish to take the real-for-sure Wishing Pebble away from me. Instead, they were very happy to think that I had the real-for-sure Wishing Pebble!"

"And I am glad you have it, too!" the old Witch laughed. "If I had known it a short time ago, probably I would have wanted it and would have tried to take it away from you. You see," the old Witch went on, "the only magical thing I have is a left-handed safety pin, and while it works lots of magic, still there are times when it will not work magic at all!"

"May I see it?" Raggedy Ann asked the old Witch.

"Certainly," the old Witch replied, as she took the left-handed safety pin out of her pocket and handed it to Raggedy Ann.

Raggedy Ann looked at the left-handed safety pin and turned it over and over. "Do you know what, Missus Witch?" Raggedy Ann asked. "I believe it is a very, very good magical left-handed safety pin, but see here! It is bent, and I'll bet a penny that is why you did not work good magic instead of unkind magic."

Then Raggedy Ann held her other hand over the left-handed safety pin for a moment and made a wish. Then, when she took her hand away, there was a right-handed safety pin lying beside the left-handed safety pin, and the left-handed safety pin wasn't bent even a smidgin.

"Now I'll bet a penny," Raggedy Ann laughed as she handed the right- and left-handed safety pins to the old

Witch, "if you work magic, you will find that it is dandy fine magic, if you work it to give pleasure to another!"

"I think so, too!" the old Witch cried. "And I thank you ever and ever so much, Raggedy Ann! Now I guess I will try and think of something real nice to magic for everyone here to enjoy!"

"Maybe if you would change the Magician's whiskers from green back to white it would make him happy!" Raggedy Ann said.

"Dear me! Has the Magician really and truly got green whiskers, Raggedy Ann?" the Witch asked. "I am colour blind! And I can not tell green from red, or any other colour!"

"Yes! His whiskers are green!" Raggedy Ann answered. "You see, when he tried to magic his whiskers and make them grow nice and long, you made his magic work lopsided, I guess. Anyway, you made his whiskers grow so long he tripped upon them. Then, when I tried to unmagic his whiskers, your magic made them turn as green as grass!"

"Then I am sorry!" the Witch said. "And the first thing I shall magic is the Magician's green whiskers! But listen, Raggedy Ann!" the old Witch whispered, and she leaned over and talked so low, Raggedy Ann could hardly hear her.

But Raggedy Ann nodded her rag head and smiled as wide as she could.

"That will be a nice thing to do!" Raggedy Ann said,

out loud. "And I'll bet it will please the Magician very, very much, for I do not believe he would wish it for himself, for fear it might be a selfish wish!"

"Then I shall do it, Raggedy Ann!" the old Witch laughed. "Won't he be surprised?"

"You bet he will!" Raggedy Ann said out loud to the old Witch. Then, to herself, she thought, "And so will you!"

For you see, whatever it was that the old Witch intended doing for the Magician, Raggedy Ann intended doing for the old Witch. So the old Witch closed her eyes and held the right- and left-handed safety pins tight in her hands and made a wish. Then, while she was doing this, Raggedy Ann made the same wish for the old Witch.

"Has the magic worked?" the old Witch asked, as she opened her eyes.

"Indeed, it has!" Raggedy Ann laughed. "Just look at the Magician now!"

"It worked fine!" the old Witch cried, as she jumped up and ran to the Magician.

Everyone stopped their fun to look at the Magician and the old Witch. For you see, the old Witch had wished for the old Magician to be changed from an old man into a young man. And Raggedy Ann had wished, at the same time, for the old Witch to be changed from an old woman into a young woman. And both wishes had come true right away.

"Whee!" the Snoopwiggy and all the woodland creatures cried.

"Unselfish wishes are the best kind of wishes!" Raggedy Ann said, when she looked at the Magician and the Witch.

"If the Witch had not wished for the old Magician to be young and handsome, then Raggedy Ann would not have wished for the old Witch to be young and pretty again!" the Snoopwiggy said to the Wiggysnoop.

"I am glad that the old Witch made the kindly wish then!" the Wiggysnoop replied. "For it is lots more fun if everyone is happy! And I'll bet now the Magician will marry the pretty Witch, just like in real-for-sure fairy tales!"

"I hadn't thought of that," the Magician said, "but I think it would be nice!"

The pretty Witch thought so, too, and so did everyone else.

"Who will we have to marry us, I wonder?" the Magician asked.

"Why not let Raggedy Andy marry you?" the Wiggysnoop asked in reply.

"Oh! I do not know how to marry anyone!" Raggedy Andy said. "Someone else will have to do it!"

"Then I will be glad to marry them!" Grinny Bear said. "For I have watched a lot of weddings!"

"Whee!" the Witch and the Magician and all the woodland creatures cried. "Grinny Bear will say the wedding ceremony! Won't that be nice?"

"First, I must have a book to read out of!" Grinny Bear said, "then I must have a lovely ring for the Magician to put on the Witch's finger!"

"I will make a lovely book!" the Witch laughed.

"And I will magic a beautiful ring!" the Magician said.

It only took the pretty Witch and the handsome Magician a minute and a half to magic the book and the beautiful diamond ring and, as everyone gathered around in a circle beneath the great forest trees, Grinny Bear pretended to read aloud from the book and, in fifteen minutes, the pretty Witch and the handsome Magician were married.

While Grinny Bear was busy marrying the pretty Witch and the handsome Magician, Raggedy Ann's cotton-stuffed head had been very busy thinking nice things. And, because she had a Candy Heart and a Wishing Pebble sewed up inside her cotton-stuffed body, Raggedy Ann could easily think of happy things.

So, just as soon as Grinny Bear had finished marrying the pretty Witch and the handsome Magician, Raggedy Ann had thought out her wish and made it come true.

Raggedy Ann's wish was this, "I wish that everyone here had a lovely, beautiful wedding present for the pretty Witch and the handsome Magician!" And sure enough everyone there walked up to the pretty Witch and the handsome Magician and handed them the presents.

There were so many presents, when everyone had done this, the pretty Witch and the handsome Magician could not carry them all. So the Magician laughed and said, "Everyone will have to bring the presents and come to my brand new white marble castle!"

So while the birds flew above them and sang, the handsome Magician and the pretty Witch led the way through the woods to where the Magician had magicked the loveliest white marble castle.

CHAPTER ELEVEN

MAGICAL WISHES COME TRUE

"IT MUST be nice to own a Wishing Pebble, or a brass button or a right- and left-handed safety pin!" the Wiggysnoop said to the Snoopwiggy as they went with the pretty Witch and the handsome Magician and Raggedy Ann and Raggedy Andy and Grinny Bear and little Neepy and all the woodland creatures into the beautiful white marble castle which the handsome Magician had made for the pretty Witch. "For with any of those magical things you can wish for such nice things!"

"I guess if I had any of those magical things, I wouldn't know what to wish for first!" the Snoopwiggy laughed.

Raggedy Ann was standing right behind the Wiggysnoop and the Snoopwiggy, when they were talking, and she thought to herself, "I'll bet it would be fun just to see what these two good friends would wish for, if they each had a wish to come true!"

So she said to the Snoopwiggy and the Wiggysnoop, "If you two might each make a wish and have it come true, what would you wish for?"

"I know what I would wish for!" the Snoopwiggy replied.

"Then," Raggedy Ann laughed, "I shall wish that you may both have a wish come true!"

"Now when I count three," Raggedy Ann said, "the Snoopwiggy shall make a wish!"

Then she called to everyone and said, "Just you all

watch and see what the Snoopwiggy is going to wish for, 'cause I have given him one wish which will come true! Then I shall give one wish to come true to the Wiggysnoop, so everyone must be real quiet, just like little baby mice!"

Of course, everyone was anxious to see what the Snoopwiggy and the Wiggysnoop would wish for, 'cause everyone felt sure that they would both make nice surprise wishes.

So the Snoopwiggy closed his eyes and wished, just as hard as he could.

When he opened his eyes, everyone shouted happily, for there right before everyone in the centre of the handsome Magician's white marble castle hall was the finest ice-cream soda-water fountain anyone could wish for. It was made of white marble trimmed in gold.

"Thank you ever and ever so much, Mister Snoopwiggy!" the handsome Magician and the pretty Witch said. "It is a lovely soda-fountain and we must all try every flavour."

So all the woodland creatures and the Raggedys and Grinny Bear and the Snoopwiggy and the Wiggysnoop and little Neepy and the pretty Witch and the handsome Magician tried every flavour and all agreed that it was the finest ice-cream soda-water they had ever tasted.

"I think your wish was just as nice as it could be, Mister Snoopwiggy!" the pretty Witch said.

"Indeed it is!" the handsome Magician added, "for now, with a beautiful white and gold soda-water fountain, right in the centre of our lovely white marble castle hall, we can have lots and lots of fun!"

"And everyone can come right in and have ice-cream sodas, whenever they wish!" the pretty Witch said.

"I am glad I thought to wish for the magical fountain!" the Snoopwiggy said, "for if you get a lot of pleasure from it, then that will make me happy, too!"

"Now!" Raggedy Ann said, "let us see what the Wiggysnoop will wish for! You know, I promised the Snoopwiggy and the Wiggysnoop that they could both have a wish which would come true!"

"Yes!" all the woodland creatures cried. "Let us see what the Wiggysnoop will wish for!"

"I shall wish for something which almost all boys and girls have wished for sometime in their lives!" the Wiggysnoop laughed. "I hope that it will please the pretty Witch and the handsome Magician, if my wish comes true!"

"Oh! we are certain it will!" the pretty Witch and the handsome Magician laughed. "Because it will be a magical wish and it is certain to be a nice one!"

So the Wiggysnoop closed his eyes, although he did not need to do it, and made his wish.

He was almost afraid to open them for fear his wish would not come true. But Raggedy Ann, because she had the magical Wishing Pebble sewed up inside her cotton-stuffed body, knew the wish, if it was a really and truly unselfish one, would come true. And sure enough it did.

When the Wiggysnoop heard everyone shout for joy, he opened his eyes and saw just what he had wished for.

At one side of the Magician's white marble castle hall was an entrance into the nicest and finest sweet shop Raggedy Ann and Raggedy Andy had ever seen, and they had seen a great many.

All the candy in the magical sweet shop was in neat white glass dishes and each dish was filled with a different kind of candy, chocolates and cream candies and every kind. There were even liquorice candies!

"And I wished that each time one of the candy dishes was emptied, that it would fill right up again!" the Wiggysnoop said, as everyone walked into the lovely place and started eating candy.

And of course, when the Raggedys and the Magician and the pretty Witch and their friends heard the Wiggysnoop say this, they knew he had spent a lot of time thinking out his wish. And, of course, it was a wish which every boy and girl has made sometime in his life. And you may be sure, the handsome Magician and his pretty Witch wife were very happy to receive such lovely presents with which they could make others happy.

All the time the Wiggysnoop and the Snoopwiggy were making their wishes, Raggedy Andy had noticed the dancing of Grinny Bear's eyes. "He is just as happy as if they had been his magical wishes!" Raggedy Andy thought. Then he walked over to Raggedy Ann and whispered, "Don't you think it would be nice for you to give nice old Grinny Bear a wish, too, Raggedy Ann?"

Raggedy Ann laughed, as she answered, "Don't you think that I had forgotten Grinny Bear, Raggedy Andy! I shall let him make his wish now!"

Then she called to Grinny Bear, "Oh Grinny Bear!" she said, "I have saved your wish until now! So you make a wish and have it come true!"

"Thank you, dear Raggedy Ann!" Grinny Bear said. "While I did not expect to make a wish, still I have thought of one!"

"Now we must all remain quiet while Grinny Bear makes his wish!" the handsome Magician laughed.

89

So everyone gathered around Grinny Bear in the great hall of the Magician's castle and Grinny Bear made his wish.

When Grinny Bear opened his eyes and smiled around at everyone, everyone turned around and looked about the great hall of the castle. Maybe they expected Grinny Bear to wish for another candy store, or another soda-water fountain.

"Now what in the world did you wish for, Grinny Bear?" everyone asked in a jumble of voices.

"We will have to go outside to see if my wish has come true!" Grinny Bear laughed. "My! I hope it has!"

So everyone ran to the great doors of the castle and looked out and when they looked out, they all had to hold their breaths in amazement.

"I knew it!" Raggedy Ann cried, her happiness making her shoe-button eyes almost jiggle off their threads. "Grinny Bear has thought his gift out to the last detail!"

The pretty Witch and the handsome Magician caught Grinny Bear and hugged him tightly, even though he wiggled and tried to get away, for this is what they saw, when they looked out of the great doors of the castle.

The castle, instead of being upon the flat ground, as it had been before, now stood upon a high island entirely surrounded with lovely blue water; pretty boats, just like beautiful birds, were sailing around far below.

And at one side of the castle was the merry-go-round and all the other wonderful things in which to have fun,

and at the other side of the castle were little houses of white marble with red roofs. And over the door of each, on a neat little sign, was the name of the woodland creature who should live there. Everyone walked around looking at the pretty houses.

"Yes, sir, Mister Grinny Bear! You have made a wonderful wish!" the pretty Witch said. "Now we can all live here happily, forever and ever just as if we were all in Fairyland!"

"Now dear little Neepy must have a wish!" Raggedy Ann said. "Have you thought of one, little Neepy?"

"I shall just wish that all of us may live here, loving each other and sharing each other's pleasures!" little Neepy said in a quiet voice. "And that this lovely place shall be invisible to all who travel through the deep, deep woods, excepting to those who have kindly, generous hearts, or to those who are in trouble and need our assistance. And"—little Neepy smiled to think of how much he was wishing at one time—"that a little white magic boat shall always meet those who visit us and bring them to our lovely island!"

"That is a beautiful wish, little Neepy," everyone cried.

Then the Wiggysnoop and the Snoopwiggy threw their hats in the air and howled ever so loudly, "Let us make little Neepy our King! Long live King Neepy!"

"Oh no!" little Neepy cried, when the two friends had stopped howling. "No one should be King! We must all be just like brothers and sisters and no one any better than another!"

"Little Neepy is quite right!" Raggedy Ann laughed.

You may be certain that the pretty Witch, the handsome Magician and the Snoopwiggy and the Wiggysnoop and Grinny Bear and little Neepy and all the woodland creatures were as happy as could be. They all cried, "Three cheers for Raggedy Ann and Raggedy Andy!"

"I know what we should do!" the handsome Magician

said, "We should name our place 'Raggedy Island,' so that whoever comes to share our happiness and pleasures will know that Raggedy Ann and Raggedy Andy have made it possible!"

The pretty Witch hugged Raggedy Andy and the Magician hugged Raggedy Ann and afterwards all the others hugged them, too, and said, "We shall always love you!"

And the Raggedys replied, "And we shall always love you, too!"

Then Raggedy Ann felt her cotton-stuffed body and everyone looked at her.

asked, as he ran to her side.

"Oh! We hope Raggedy Ann is not going to be ill!" the little woodland creatures cried.

"Oh no!" the pretty Witch said, "Raggedy Ann cannot be ill! But tell us, dear Raggedy Ann!"

"It's the magical Wishing Pebble!" Raggedy Ann replied. "It is jiggling around in my cotton-stuffed body, and I am sure it wishes me to know something!"

"Now we must all remain very quiet, while Raggedy Ann wishes to know why the magical Wishing Pebble jiggles!" Raggedy Andy said, as he held up his rag hand for silence.

Everyone remained quiet while Raggedy Ann covered her shoe-button eyes with her hands.

Then, when she took her hands away, everyone could see that both shoe-button eyes were quite wet.

"I am sorry in one way, and happy in another!" Raggedy Ann said in her soft cottony voice. "Raggedy Andy and I must leave at once! Marcella has reached home and, remembering that she left Raggedy Andy and me in the little play-house out in the garden, she is anxious to find us there, safe and sound! The time is short, we cannot even kiss you all goodbye, but you must know how much we shall always love you!"

And Raggedy Ann caught hold of Raggedy Andy's hand and, covering her eyes, she made the wish to be in the play-house immediately.

And, as she and Raggedy Andy found themselves there, they seemed to hear a faint chorus of all their friends crying, "And we shall always love YOU!"

But Raggedy Ann and Andy had no time to say anything, for Marcella was running down the path through the orchard, as fast as she could run.

She threw aside the door covering and caught the two loppy rag dolls in her arms and as she ran up towards the house with them she said, "I forgot and left you there until mama and I were almost in town, then it was too late, but, oh dear, I was afraid something would happen to you." Then she laughed softly, "And I had all my fright for nothing, Mama," as she walked into the house. "The dear old Raggedys had not moved at all, all the time we were away!"

And Raggedy Ann and Raggedy Andy wiggled their shoe-button eyes at each other, as much to say, "Ha, ha, ha! Is that so?"

THE END